IMAGINE THAT

Licensed exclusively to Imagine That Publishing Ltd
Tide Mill Way, Woodbridge, Suffolk, IP12 1AP, UK
www.imaginethat.com
Copyright © 2020 Imagine That Group Ltd
All rights reserved
9
Manufactured in China

Written by Amber Lily
Illustrated by Richard Merritt

ISBN 978-1-78958-482-0

A catalogue record for this book is available from the British Library

Little UNicorN LearNS to DaNCe

Written by Amber Lily
Illustrated by Richard Merritt

It was an important day for Little Unicorn.
She was going to a ballet class for the very first time!

Little Unicorn was nervous about learning to dance …
she was scared that she would get her hooves muddled up!

Little Unicorn was trotting through the forest, practising twirling and whirling, when she saw Little Fairy walking towards her.

'I'm learning to fly!' said Little Fairy.
'Are you scared?' asked Little Unicorn.
'Not really. I'm not very good yet, but I can almost get off the ground,' said Little Fairy, proudly.

Little Unicorn continued along the path to her ballet class. Suddenly, she saw a shower of magic sparkles falling on the path ahead.

High above her, in the sky, was Little Fairy, swooping and loop-the-looping through the air. 'I'm flying!' Little Fairy shouted, happily.

Little Unicorn trotted on, practising twirling and whirling as she went. Suddenly she heard a splash and Little Mermaid jumped up on the path beside her. 'I'm learning to swim!' said Little Mermaid, happily. 'Are you scared?' asked Little Unicorn.

'Not really. I'm not very good yet, but I can almost swim across the pool, and it's lots of fun!' Little Mermaid saw some other mermaids swim past, so she plunged back into the water.

Trotting on, Little Unicorn heard an excited shout.
'Look, Little Unicorn!' cried Little Mermaid.
'I can swim right across the pool!'

Little Mermaid was very pleased and swam off to show her other friends.

Little Unicorn was getting close to her ballet class and so she stopped for a little rest. As she was resting, a big puff of smoke blew past. 'Sorry, Little Unicorn,' said Little Dragon. 'I'm learning to breathe fire.'

'Are you scared?' asked Little Unicorn. 'Not really. So far, I've only blown smoke rings, but I can almost do it,' said Little Dragon, blowing out a puff of smoke.

As Little Unicorn started to make her way to the ballet class again, she saw fiery sprinkles shoot across the sky. It was Little Dragon, breathing fire at last!

'Look at this one!' roared Little Dragon, as he blew enormous flames up into the air.

Little Unicorn was still worrying about how to twirl her legs and whirl her hooves.

She could see all of her friends
having fun, learning new things.

Little Unicorn trotted up to the door of her ballet class, took a deep breath and went in. She put on her tutu and ballet slippers, but she didn't want to dance.

Then she thought about her friends and how they were not scared to learn new things. Little Unicorn wanted to be brave, too!

As the music started to play,
Little Unicorn took a deep breath
and listened to the tune.

Little Unicorn twirled her legs and whirled around on her hooves and she was ...

'Amazing! Look, it's a tutu-nicorn!' clapped the ballet teacher as she watched Little Unicorn dance gracefully around the room.

Little Unicorn had learnt that it is good to try new things.

Even though she had been nervous, Little Unicorn could not wait to come back and dance again tomorrow!

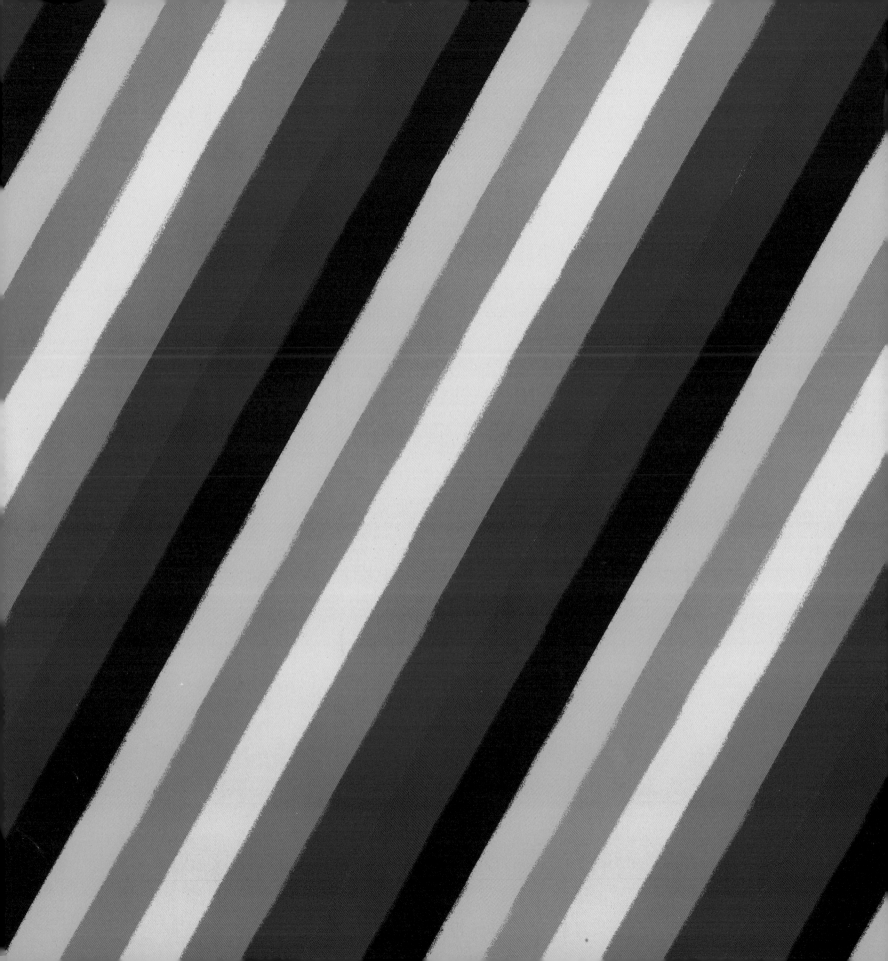

university for the **creative arts**

PRIN CD P G

LOEWY: LONDON

RotoVision

A ROTOVISION BOOK \\\\\ \\\\\\\\\\\\\\\\\\\\\\\\\ PUBLISHED AND DISTRIBUTED BY ROTOVISION SA, ROUTE SUISSE 9, CH-1295 MIES, SWITZERLAND \\\\\ \\\\\\ \\\\\\\\\\\\\\\\\\\\\\\\\\\\\\\\\\ ROTOVISION SA, SALES & EDITORIAL OFFICE: SHERIDAN HOUSE, 114 WESTERN ROAD, HOVE BN3 1DD, UK \\\ \\\\\\\\\\\\\\\\\\\\\\\\\\\\\\\\\ TEL: +44 (0)1273 727268, FAX: +44 (0)1273 727269, WEB: WWW.ROTOVISION.COM \\\\\ \\\\\\\\\\\\\\\\\\\\\ \\\\\\\\\ \\\\\\\\\ \\\\\\\\\\\\\\\\\\\\\ COPYRIGHT © ROTOVISION SA 2009 \\\\\\\\\\\\\\\\\\\\\\\\\\\\\\\ \\\\\\\\\\\\ \\\ \\\\\\\\\\\\\\\\\\\\\\

\\\\\\\\\\\\\\\\\\\\\\\\\\\\\\\\\\\\\\ 10 9 8 7 6 5 4 3 2 1 \\ \\ ISBN-13: 978-2-88893-056-3 \\\ ROTOVISION ART DIRECTOR: TONY SEDDON \\\ \\\\\\\\\\\\\\\\\\\\\\\\\\\\\\\\\\\\\\\ WRITTEN+DESIGNED AT LOEWY: LONDON [+44 (0)20 7798 2000] \\\ \\ \\\\\\ REPROGRAPHICS IN SINGAPORE BY PROVISION PTE. \\ \\\ PRINTED IN SINGAPORE BY STAR STANDARD INDUSTRIES (PTE.) LTD